In a high-rise building
deep in the heart of a big city
live two private eyes:
Bunny Brown and Jack Jones.
Bunny is the brains,
Jack is the snoop,
and together they
crack cases wide open . . .

This is the story of
Case Number 001:
THE CASE OF
THE MISSING MONKEY

story by
Cynthia Rylant

pictures by
G. Brian Karas

THE
HIGH-RISE
PRIVATE
EYES

The High-Rise Private Eyes

The Case of the
Missing Monkey

HarperCollinsPublishers

To Ben Frederick
—C.R.

For the Little Feet Library
—G.B.K.

Acrylic, gouache, and pencil were used for the full-color art.
The text type is Times.

HarperCollins®, 🐿®, and I Can Read Book® are
trademarks of HarperCollins Publishers Inc.

The High-Rise Private Eyes: The Case of the Missing Monkey
Text copyright © 2000 by Cynthia Rylant
Illustrations copyright © 2000 by G. Brian Karas
Manufactured in China. All rights reserved.
For information address HarperCollins Children's Books,
a division of HarperCollins Publishers,
10 East 53rd Street, New York, NY 10022.
www.harperchildrens.com

Library of Congress Cataloging-in-Publication Data
Rylant, Cynthia.
    The high-rise private eyes : the case of the missing monkey /
by Cynthia Rylant ; illustrated by G. Brian Karas.
        p.   cm. — (An I can read book)
    "Greenwillow Books."
    Summary: While having breakfast at their favorite diner,
two detectives, Bunny and Jack, solve a mystery that is not
what it seems.
    ISBN 0-688-16306-8 — ISBN 0-688-16305-X (lib. bdg.)
    ISBN 0-06-444306-X (pbk.)
    [l. Animals—Fiction. 2. Mystery and detective stories.]
I. Karas, G. Brian, ill. II. Title.
PZ7.R982 Ho 2000   99-16878
[E]—dc21   CIP

14 15 16 17 18 SCP 20 19 18 17

❖

Originally published by Greenwillow Books, an imprint of
HarperCollins Publishers, in 2000.

Contents

B unny liked brussels sprouts
and cheese for breakfast
every morning.

"Yuck," said Jack.

"It's delicious. Try some,"
said Bunny.

7

"Just the cheese," said Jack.

"Have a brussels sprout," said Bunny.

"No," said Jack.

"Just one," said Bunny.

"No!" said Jack.

"Just a teeny one," said Bunny.

"NO!" said Jack.

"Why not?" asked Bunny.

"BECAUSE I HATE

BRUSSELS SPROUTS!"

said Jack.

"How do you know?" asked Bunny.

"I just know," said Jack.

"How?" asked Bunny.

"I just DO!" said Jack.

"Ha," said Bunny.

Suddenly Jack had an idea.

He picked up a potted plant.

"Here," said Jack. "Have a bite."

"What?" asked Bunny.

"Just one," said Jack.

"No!" said Bunny.

"Just a teeny one," said Jack.

"NO!" said Bunny.

"Why not?" asked Jack.

"BECAUSE I HATE
POTTED PLANTS!"
said Bunny.

"How do you know?" asked Jack.

Bunny looked at Jack.

Jack looked at Bunny.

"Let's go out for pancakes,"
said Bunny.

"Good idea," said Jack.

Chapter 2
The Case

Bunny and Jack went
to their favorite diner,
The Grill Next Door.

Mac, the owner of the grill,

saw them.

"Bunny! Jack!" he said.

"I'm so glad to see you!

I need your help!"

"What's up?" said Jack.

"The monkey is missing!" said Mac.

"Eeeeeeek!" screamed Bunny.

Jack and Mac looked at Bunny.

"Gee, I didn't know

you liked monkeys that much,"

said Jack.

"No, it's not that.

It's THIS!" cried Bunny.

She held up a finger.

"My nail's broken," she said.

(Bunny could be a bit vain.)

"It was my favorite," said Bunny.

"How can you have
a favorite fingernail?" asked Jack.

"Well, I can," said Bunny.

"DOES ANYBODY CARE
ABOUT MY MONKEY?"
wailed Mac.
"Oh. Sorry, Mac," said Jack.
"Give us the details."

17

"Okay," said Mac. "Start writing."
And he gave Bunny and Jack
the details:

> 1 glass monkey next to
>   cash register at 8 A.M.
> Gone at 9 A.M.

Jack looked at Mac.
"That's it?" he asked.
"That's it," said Mac.

"But who was in the grill at 8 A.M.?"
asked Bunny.

She loved a case.

She forgot all about her nail.

"Just the regulars," said Mac.

"The regulars," repeated Bunny,
writing it down.

"Which means they'll be here again
tomorrow at 8 A.M.?" asked Jack.
"Right," said Mac.
"Good. Then I'll have
a strawberry pancake
and a glass of OJ,"
said Jack.

"Me too," said Bunny.

"What about my monkey?" asked Mac.

"Whoever took it

will be back here tomorrow,"

said Bunny.

"And so will we.

Then we'll solve the case."

"In the meantime, we'll have pancakes,"
said Jack. "But no brussels sprouts."
"And no potted plants either,"
said Bunny.

Mac looked at them both.

"Not on the menu," he said.

"Well, thank goodness," said Jack.

Chapter 3
Suspects

Bunny and Jack were back

at The Grill Next Door

early the next morning.

"Mmmmmm," said Jack.

"Smell those pancakes cooking."

"Concentrate, Jack," said Bunny.

"We're on the job now."

"Okay," said Jack.

Jack looked at a fox

sitting in one corner.

"One fox," he said.

"One book being read by fox.

And—oh, boy—

are those *chocolate chip* pancakes

he's eating?"

Bunny wrote down:

1 fox with book

Jack looked in the other corner.

"Okay," he said.

"One crow with one bag.

And he's eating—oh, yummy—

powdered doughnuts."

Bunny wrote down:

1 crow with bag

Jack looked at the counter.

"Okay, listen up," Jack told Bunny.

"There's a moose with a mouse,

a bear with a hare,

and a dog with a frog."

Bunny looked up from her notepad.

"What?" she asked.

At the counter she saw only

a sheep with a lunchbox.

Jack grinned.

"I feel poetic today," he said.

Bunny made a face and wrote down:

1 sheep with lunchbox
1 corny private eye

Jack saw what Bunny wrote.

"Am not," he said.

"Are too," said Bunny.

"Not," said Jack.

"Too," said Bunny.

"I'm just very, very clever,"
said Jack. "Like a fox."
Bunny waited.
"Like a fox with a box,"
said Jack.
Bunny groaned.

Chapter 4
Solved

As Bunny and Jack were talking,

Mac stepped out of the kitchen.

"Bunny! Jack!" He waved.

He came closer to them.

"Did you find the monkey?"

he whispered.

"No."

"Yes."

Bunny and Jack looked at each other.

"You solved it already?"
asked Jack.

"Sure," said Bunny.

"How?" said Jack.

"Well," said Bunny, "if you hadn't
been looking at everybody's food,
you'd have solved it too."

She pointed to the corner.

"There's a fox reading
a book on trains.
That fox likes big machines,
not delicate little monkeys.
He's not our guy."

"Okay," said Jack. "Go on."

"There's a sheep at the counter.

His lunchbox has a million dents in it.

That sheep is too clumsy

to want something made of glass.

He's not our guy," said Bunny.

"Okay, again," said Jack.

"Then there's the crow in the corner with the baby tote," said Bunny.

"That's a baby tote?" asked Jack.

"Sure—see the bottle in the pouch?" asked Bunny.

"Right," said Jack.

"And I'll bet there's a baby crow
in that bag. And I'll bet
that's the papa crow," said Bunny.
Jack's eyes got big.
"Now I get it!" said Jack.
"The papa needs to keep the baby quiet
so he can eat!"

38

"Right," said Bunny.

"And what do crows love?"

"*Shiny* stuff!" said Mac.

"Hey, you took my line," said Jack.

"Oops, sorry," said Mac.

"I'll bet the crow borrowed
the glass monkey yesterday
to keep the baby happy.

"He just forgot to put it back,"
said Bunny.
"But I'll bet he sets that monkey
on the table when he leaves."
"Nothing to do but wait and eat,"
said Jack. "Mac, what's cooking?"

Jack and Bunny sat down
at the counter.
They ate and talked with Mac

until the sheep left,

the fox left,

and finally the crow left.

"Check the table!" said Bunny.

Jack went over to the crow's table.

He held up the glass monkey

for Bunny and Mac to see.

"Hooray!" said Mac.

"Case closed," said Bunny.

"He even left a doughnut," said Jack.

"I love a thief
with a small appetite."

"Not a thief," said Bunny.

"A borrower."

"Right," said Jack.

He held out the doughnut to Bunny.

"Want it?" he asked.

"No, thanks," she said.

"Just one bite," said Jack.

"No," said Bunny.

"Just a teeny one," said Jack.

"NO!" said Bunny.

"Why not?" said Jack.

Jack looked at her.

"BECAUSE I . . ." Bunny began.

She stopped.

She looked at Jack.

Then they laughed and laughed.

"Here we go again!" Jack said.